The children were dipping
strawberries into chocolate.
"They look yummy!" said Chip.
"They taste yummy!" said Kipper.

Kipper went to Biff's room. He had
chocolate on his hands. He got
chocolate on everything he touched.
"Go away, Kipper!" said Biff.

"You're getting chocolate on everything," said Chip.

"I wish everything I touched turned into chocolate," said Kipper.

"That's just greedy," said Chip.

Just then the magic key began to glow. It took the children into an adventure.

They saw a girl sitting by a river.
She was crying.
"What's the matter?" asked Biff.

"Come with me and I'll show you,"
said the girl. "My name is Zoe."
Zoe took them to a palace.

The children gasped. The palace
was made of gold, and a gold tree
stood outside.

Zoe took the children inside.
Everything was made of gold, even
the food on the table!

"My father is King Midas," said
Zoe sadly. "He made a wish that
everything he touched turned into
gold. Now his wish has come true!"

"If the food turns into gold, how can he eat it?" asked Chip.

"He can't," said Zoe. "And if he touches me, I'll turn into gold too."

Just then King Midas came in.
Zoe hid behind Biff. "My father
used to hug me," she said, "but he
mustn't do it anymore."

King Midas saw Floppy. "I love
dogs," he said. "Come here!"

"Stop!" called Chip. "Don't touch that dog!"

It was too late. King Midas patted Floppy and he turned into gold.

"I'm so sorry," said King Midas. "I forgot that everything I touch turns into gold. I wish I could turn him back into a real dog again."

"Who granted the wish?" asked
Biff.

"It was Dionysus," said the king.

"Then we must go and see him,"
said Biff, "and ask him to help."

Dionysus lived on Mount Olympus.
It was a long way to walk, but at last
King Midas and the children arrived.

"Why have you come back to see me?" asked Dionysus.

"I have come to ask you to help me," said King Midas.

"I want everything back the way it was," said King Midas. "My wish was silly."

"You were foolish and greedy," said Dionysus. "But you have learnt your lesson. Now go back and do what I tell you."

Dionysus told them to get water from the river. They had to pour it onto everything that had turned into gold.

"It works!" said King Midas. "I'm so glad your dog is back."

"So am I!" said Kipper.

King Midas gave Zoe a hug.
"What a fool I have been," he said.
"I'm glad I can hug you now. I will
never ask for gold again!"

King Midas looked at the children.
"Thank you for helping us," he said.
The key began to glow. It was
time to go home.

"Hey! Why did you do that?"
asked Kipper, crossly.

"To stop you from turning into
chocolate," laughed Chip.

Think about the story

Why was Zoe crying?

How was Floppy turned into gold?

Why was King Midas's wish foolish and greedy?

What would you wish for?

Matching pairs

Match each water carrier with his gold twin.

Useful common words repeated in this story and other
books in the series.

asked   children   chocolate   everything   gold   just   made
now   took   turned

Names in this story: Biff   Chip   Dionysus   Floppy   Kipper
King Midas   Olympus   Zoe